The Messy Cake

Sue Graves

W

A story in a familiar setting

First published in 2011 by
Franklin Watts
338 Euston Road
London NW1 3BH

Franklin Watts Australia
Level 17/207 Kent Street
Sydney NSW 2000

A CIP catalogue record for this book is
available from the British Library.

ISBN: 978 1 4451 0408 9 (hbk)
ISBN: 978 1 4451 0416 4 (pbk)

Illustrations by Artful Doodlers Ltd.
Art Director: Jonathan Hair
Series Editor: Jackie Hamley
Series Designer: Matthew Lilly

Printed in China

Franklin Watts is a division of
Hachette Children's Books,
an Hachette UK company.
www.hachette.co.uk

Kim wanted to bake a cake.

"Be careful," said Mum.

"Try not to make a mess!"

Sal and Ash came over to help.
"We mustn't make a mess!"
said Kim.

Kim carefully mixed together
some butter and sugar in a bowl.

Ash carefully cracked
some eggs into
the mixture.

Sal carefully sifted in some flour.

Kim carefully whisked
it all together.

Kim and Sal poured the
mixture into the cake tin.

Dad helped put the
cake tin in the oven.
Nobody made
any mess.

Soon the cake was ready.
Dad took it out of the oven and
put it onto the rack to cool.

"Let's put some icing
on the cake," said Sal.
"Yes but don't make a mess!"
said Kim and Ash.

Sal put the icing on the cake.
She didn't spill a drop.

Kim put the cake on a big plate. Then he carefully carried it into the living room to show Mum.

"Look at the cake, Mum.
And we didn't make any mess
at all!" said Kim.

"Well done!" said Mum.
Then, suddenly, the cake
began to slide...

"Oh, no!" said Kim.

"We didn't make a mess!"

"No!" said Mum. "You didn't. But I made a huge mess! Sorry!"

Puzzles

Which speech bubbles
belong to Kim?

Put the sentences in order
to retell the story.

Sal and Ash helped
Kim make the cake.

Kim wanted to make a cake.

Mum said, "Don't
make a mess."

Mum dropped the cake
and made a mess.

Sal put icing on the cake.

Answers

Kim's speech bubbles are: 1, 4

The order of the story is:

Kim wanted to make a cake.

Mum said, "Don't make a mess."

Sal and Ash helped Kim make the cake.

Sal put icing on the cake.

Mum dropped the cake and made a mess.

Espresso Connections

This book may be used in conjunction with the English area on Espresso to promote group discussion and start an activity on writing instructions. Here are some suggestions.

Group discussion

Visit the Storyboards section in Speaking and Listening, English 1, and open either Packing a lunchbox (for approximately five steps) or Easter Bunny (for more steps).

Watch the video and ask the children to think about the steps in which things happen.

Then ask them to talk about these steps in small groups, and to write these steps out as a set of instructions.

Writing Instructions

Now, ask children to think of another activity that requires a set of steps, for example making a card or cleaning out a pet home. They should be able to choose the activity they want to write about.

Ask them to write out the instructions for completing their chosen activity. Remind them to think about what they need to complete the activity and the order in which the steps must happen.